D0910009

The Cuckoo Child

By the same author

DODOS ARE FOREVER
GEORGE SPEAKS
PADDY'S POT OF GOLD
THE WATER HORSE

DICK KING-SMITH

The
Cuckoo Child

Illustrated by David Parkins

WINDSOR PUBLIC LIBRARY

VIKING

VIKING

Published by the Penguin Group
Penguin Books Ltd, 27 Wrights Lane, London w8 5tz, England
Viking Penguin, a division of Penguin Books USA Inc.
375 Hudson Street, New York, New York 10014, USA
Penguin Books Australia Ltd, Ringwood, Victoria, Australia
Penguin Books Canada Ltd, 2801 John Street, Markham, Ontario, Canada l3r 1b4
Penguin Books (NZ) Ltd, 182–190 Wairau Road, Auckland 10, New Zealand

Penguin Books Ltd, Registered Offices: Harmondsworth, Middlesex, England

First published 1991
1 3 5 7 9 10 8 6 4 2

Text copyright © Fox Busters Limited, 1991
Illustrations copyright © David Parkins, 1991

The moral right of the author has been asserted

All rights reserved. Without limiting the rights under copyright reserved above,
no part of this publication may be reproduced, stored in or introduced into a
retrieval system, or transmitted, in any form or by any means (electronic,
mechanical, photocopying, recording or otherwise), without the prior written
permission of both the copyright owner and the above publisher of this book

Printed in England by Clays Ltd, St Ives plc
Filmset in Baskerville

A CIP catalogue record for this book is available from the British Library

ISBN 0–670– 83295–2

MAIN LIBRARY

Contents

CHAPTER I

Scrambled Eggs

'Are you warm enough?' said Jack's mother as she tucked him up in bed. Jack nodded. After his mother had kissed him good night and gone out, leaving the bedroom door ajar, he waited, listening.

He heard her footsteps going down the stairs and along the hallway to the kitchen, and then he sat up.

Twisting round, he lifted his pillows. Beneath them were three brown eggs.

'Are you warm enough?' said Jack.

Of all the animals on his father's farm, Jack liked the birds best. Farmer Daw's pride and joy was his herd of dairy cows, Mrs Daw was particularly fond of the pigs, and Jack's big sister Margery was mad on horses. But Jack's favourite creatures were birds.

Even as a helpless baby in his pram he had gurgled with pleasure at the sight of the swallows darting across the summer sky, or the sound of a sparrow's cheep or a starling's whistle. And once he was old enough to stagger about the farm, he always made straight for the poultry – the hens, the ducks,

the geese and the turkeys. Anything with feathers fascinated little Jack Daw.

Now, at four years of age, Jack was beginning to understand how birds are born. Eggs, he now knew, weren't just for people to eat. If you left them with the mother bird, and she kept them warm, baby chicks would hatch out of them. Jack wasn't too sure how this happened or how long it took.

'But I'll keep you warm all right,' he said to the three eggs. 'Don't you worry about that.'

Gently, he put the pillows back on top of them.

Carefully, he laid his head on top of the pillows.

Happily, he went to sleep.

At first Jack Daw slept peacefully, but some time later in the night he had a strange dream. In it he found an egg, not an ordinary-sized egg but a huge thing eight inches long, and out of it there hatched the strangest-looking baby bird that began to grow with nightmarish speed.

Before you could say 'Jack Daw', let alone 'Jack Robinson', the dream-chick's size increased until it stood half as tall again as a man, and stared down at him out of huge brown eyes.

Jack tossed and turned in his sleep as the nightmare gripped him, twisting his head from side to side on the pillows, until at last he woke. He looked wildly around, and then, seeing to his great relief the familiar outlines of his own safe room, fell fast asleep again.

'Jack!' his mother called next morning. 'Are you awake? Breakfast is nearly ready.'

Jack Daw lay still for a moment, remembering his dream, and then, and only then, remembering what lay beneath his pillows.

He lifted them and saw, on the sheet beneath, a horrid sticky mess of shattered shell and slimy white and gooey golden yolk.

He heard his mother's voice again.

'Hurry up!' she called. 'Or it'll spoil. It's scrambled eggs.'

CHAPTER 2

Lydia and Wilfred

At the time, Jack's mother was very angry, first with Jack, then with her husband for laughing, then with Margery for teasing Jack and then with Jack for kicking Margery. Finally, when Farmer Daw had gone out to see to his cows, and Margery Daw had gone off to school, and Jack Daw had stumped off to tell the hens and ducks and geese and turkeys how unfair life was, Mrs Daw was angry with herself for making such a fuss.

All the same, while her son was cleaning his teeth that evening, she couldn't resist having a peep under his pillows. But there was nothing there. Jack had a clean sheet.

'That boy and his birds!' she said to her husband later. 'Most children his age want animals like rabbits or guinea-pigs. Jack spends all his time in the hen-run or by the duckpond or out in the orchard with the geese and the turkeys.'

'If it's got feathers, Jack likes it,' said Farmer Daw. 'But he's got a lot to learn. Trying to hatch eggs out under his pillow overnight when it takes a hen three weeks! Time he had a lesson in chick rearing.'

And next morning, with Jack watching his every move like a hawk, he set a broody hen on a clutch of a dozen eggs.

Every day then for the next twenty-one days, father and son went together to the broody-coop to take the hen off the eggs for ten minutes, so that she could stretch her legs and make herself comfortable and have a feed of corn and a drink of water. Jack was too small to lift the fluffed-out grumbling broody off the nest by himself, but he wasn't a bit scared of her, the farmer noticed, nor of the cockerel or any of the other poultry.

'Mind she doesn't peck you,' he said, as Jack stroked the broody's ruffled feathers, but she never did.

When they came to the coop on the morning of the twenty-first day, Jack's father said, 'Listen.'

Jack listened, and heard not just the clucking of the hen but a lot of little cheeping sounds. He peered in through the bars and could see some little faces already peeping out from beneath the broody's skirts.

As luck would have it, it was a perfect hatch, for when, in the afternoon, the broody was taken out of the coop, there in a mess of broken shells were a dozen tiny fluffy chicks.

'Count them, Jack,' said Farmer Daw.

'One, two, three,' said Jack, 'five, seven, eight, nine, ten, twelve, thirteen, fifteen, sixteen.'

His father laughed, stroking the bird in his arms.

'Didn't she do well?' he said. 'You know, I don't

think you could have hatched your eggs even if you'd stayed in bed for three weeks and kept very still.'

Very carefully, Jack picked up one of the baby chicks. He held it in front of his face and stared at it, fascinated.

'Daddy,' he said, 'when can I have some birds of my very own?'

'When you're five,' said his father.

Jack's fifth birthday present was a pair of budgerigars.

For his sixth he was given bantams.

For his seventh, ducks.

All of these throve and multiplied.

Just as some people are specially skilled with plants – have 'green fingers', as they say, so that everything in their gardens does well – so Jack was good with birds. He had a way with them.

He looked after his budgies and his bantams and his ducks with great care, and they in their turn seemed anxious to do their very best for him. Other people's birds might sit on eggs that turned out to be infertile and addled, or their chicks might be dead-in-shell. But Jack's mother birds, of any sort, scarcely ever lost a baby.

One morning the Daw family were sitting at the breakfast table, eating boiled eggs (except for Jack: for some years now he had not been able to bring himself to do such a thing).

'You'll soon be eight,' said his mother.

'Yes,' said Jack.

'How about something different for a birthday present this time?' said his father.

'No,' said Jack.

'You and your birds!' said his sister Margery. 'The older you get, the bigger they get. Budgies, bantams, ducks, I suppose it'll be geese next.'

'Yes,' said Jack. 'A pair. Please.'

'But we've got four geese out in the orchard as it is,' said his father.

'That's just it,' said Jack. 'We've got four ancient old grey geese to graze the grass under the apple trees. But we haven't got a gander.'

'So what?' said Margery.

Jack sighed.

'To have babies you need a daddy as well as a mummy,' he said in a patient voice. 'Didn't you know?'

So on New Year's Day, which was Jack's birthday, a handsome young white gander and a beautiful young white goose arrived at the farm.

The gander was very protective of his mate, and stretched his neck and flapped his wings and hissed angrily if anyone came near her or indeed near the four old grey geese in the orchard. Anyone, that is, except Jack. Unafraid as usual, he won their confidence straight away, and Wilfred and Lydia, as he named them, were soon feeding from his hand and following everywhere at his heels with harsh cries of pleasure.

A couple of months later, Lydia began to make a nest in the corner of an old shed that stood under one of the apple trees. She made it of grass and hay and straw, and lined it with soft down plucked from her breast.

And then one day Jack came rushing in, grinning all over his face.

'Lydia's laid her first egg!' he said.

'A golden one, I suppose?' said Margery.

Jack sighed.

'That was just a fairy tale,' he said in a patient voice. 'Didn't you know?'

'I expect that's the biggest egg you've ever seen in your life,' said his father.

'Or ever will, I should think,' said his mother.

But there she was wrong.

The very next day, just at the moment when Lydia was laying the second of her clutch, Jack Daw was staring open-mouthed at a couple of dozen of the biggest eggs in the world!

CHAPTER 3

Then There Were Eight

For weeks the boys and girls in Jack's class at school had been excited about a planned outing to the Wildlife Park. Most of them were fond of animals anyway, and every one of them was looking forward to the coach ride, and to eating their packed lunches, and to spending their pocket-money on all kinds of attractive and useless things in the souvenir shop.

Jack felt slightly differently.

Not that he didn't want to see the white rhinos and the giraffes and the zebras and the monkeys and all the other four-legged creatures. He just wished that the class could have gone instead to Birdland or to the Tropical Bird Gardens. The Wildlife Park, he suspected, would not have many of his feathered friends.

In fact, when they arrived and began to walk around, he realized that there were more birds than he had thought; there were peacocks that roamed the grounds, macaws that flew freely among the trees, and a flock of flamingos in a lake.

The children walked along, ceaselessly nagging their teacher to allow them to open their packed lunches ('I'm starving, Miss, it's more than two hours since I had my breakfast') until they came to a point where, in a little wooded area, the path forked. Everyone took the right-hand way, except Jack who was dawdling along at the back, day-dreaming about Lydia and the chances of her laying a second egg today. Now, attracted by the sight of a peacock displaying, he took the left fork.

For a moment he stood with his back to a tall wire fence, watching the peacock, and then suddenly something told him that he himself was being watched. Slowly he turned, and there on the other side of the fence stood a great black-and-white bird half as tall again as a man, staring down at him out of huge brown eyes.

For a long moment they gazed at one another, the small boy and the great male ostrich. Then the spell was broken, as Jack heard his name angrily called, and saw his teacher beckoning to him from the fork in the paths.

'How many times do you have to be told, Jack?' she said when he reached her. 'Keep together, d'you hear me?'

'Yes, Miss,' said Jack. 'But please, Miss, we've missed the ostriches, Miss.'

The teacher looked at her map of the Wildlife Park.

'No, we haven't,' she said. 'We shall come to them later, after the rhinos.'

Jack paid little attention to the rhinos, nor did he any longer think of Lydia. His mind was full of that magnificent giant bird, of its black feathering with white wing- and tail-plumes, of its massive legs and huge two-toed feet, of its long long neck and of those great brown heavily lashed eyes that had stared into his own with such a look of intelligence and understanding. He couldn't wait to see it again!

At last they came, by the correct route, to a sign that said

| TO THE OSTRICHES ➡ |

and fixed beside it was a printed notice.

The teacher made the children stop, and she read it out to them.

OSTRICH (*Struthio camelus*)

The world's largest bird. The ostrich cannot fly, but can run at speeds of up to 40 m.p.h. Male ostriches can reach a height of 9 feet, and weigh as much as 345 pounds. Females are smaller. The male is black-and-white, the female brownish. This colour difference is an advantage when brooding eggs, for the hen bird sits on them by day, the cock by night. An ostrich egg can be 8 inches in length and 6 inches in diameter, and its shell can support the weight of a 20-stone man.

As the teacher finished reading, there was a gabble of voices.

'Nine feet high! That's half as tall again as my dad!'

'Three hundred and forty-five pounds! That's about three times as heavy as my mum!'

'My Uncle George weighs about twenty stone – fancy him balancing on an egg!'

Amidst all the noise, Jack pulled at the teacher's sleeve.

'Miss, Miss!' he said. 'D'you think we shall see an ostrich's egg?' and a man's voice answered, 'You'll see lots of them. In fact, if you hang on a few minutes, I'll bring you some and show them to you.'

Everybody looked round, and there was one of the Wildlife Park's rangers. He was pushing a small rubber-tyred barrow containing some cabbages and some apples, and he walked off, saying, 'Come on, children, follow me.'

As soon as they reached the ostrich paddock, they could see the eggs. There were a couple of dozen of them, lying on the ground in a rough scooped-out hollow made in a patch of bare earth. Even the facts given on the notice had not really prepared the children for the size of the great yellowish-white things.

'There!' said the ranger. 'How'd you like one of them for your breakfast, eh? There's as much in one of them as in twenty-four hens' eggs!'

The children gaped.

Jack put his hand up.

'Please,' he said, 'why isn't one of the ostriches sitting on them?'

'Now that's a good question, young man,' said the ranger (and Jack's teacher looked pleased), 'and I'll tell you the answer. We've got four ostriches here, three hens and a cock, and all the hens are laying at present, all in this same spot. And any day now I'm expecting one of them to go broody, and then she'll gather about fifteen of these eggs together and start sitting on them. Like it tells you on the notice, she'll sit by day and the cock bird will take over at night.'

'But what about the other eggs?' asked Jack's teacher. 'There are more than fifteen there.'

'That's a good question, Miss,' said the ranger (and Jack's teacher looked even more pleased), 'and I'll tell you the answer. I pick 'em up. The three hens lay such a lot at this time of year that if I didn't take some away, the broody bird might try to sit on too many, more than she or her mate could cover properly, and then none of them would be properly incubated. So every now and then I pick up the surplus ones.'

While the man had been talking, the four ostriches had come striding up from a distant part of the paddock, and now the great nine-foot male and his slightly smaller brown females stood by the wire, staring down.

'But don't the birds object,' said the teacher, 'if you take some of the eggs?'

'They might, Miss,' said the ranger, 'and a kick from an ostrich can kill a man, so I don't take any chances. If you and the children just stay here and watch, you'll see.'

So they stayed and watched as the ranger walked off pushing his barrow, while the four ostriches paced along inside the wire, their huge eyes fixed on the cabbages and apples.

When he had gone some way away, the ranger stopped, and began to throw the fruit and vegetables over the wire. Then, leaving the birds busily feeding, he hurried back, unlocked a wire gate in the fencing, and, pushing in the barrow, reloaded it, this time with the more outlying of the ostrich eggs.

Jack watched all this with mounting excitement. It might take a bird to hatch eggs, but a boy could hatch a plan! He loosened the zip on the canvas holdall slung over his shoulder in which he carried his lunch-box.

The ranger came out again and relocked the wire gate.

In the barrow were nine eggs.

He picked one up.

'Now,' he said, 'where's the young man that asked that question?' and when Jack put his hand up, the ranger said, 'Here, you can have first go,' and handed him an ostrich egg.

Then, one after another, he took the other spare eggs out of the barrow and gave them to various children to hold and examine.

'Let me!' 'Let me!' 'Give it here!' 'Let's have a go!' cried all the boys and girls as they competed to hold an egg, and in the hubbub and confusion nobody noticed what Jack was doing or heard him zip his holdall shut.

'Now now, children, that's enough!' said the teacher. 'Put all the eggs back in the barrow now,' and to the ranger she said, 'What will you do with these?'

'Often we send some to other safari parks or zoos,' said the ranger, 'but actually these ones today will be fed to our big snakes, the pythons and the boa constrictors. Now then, have you all put your eggs back?'

'Yes!' chorused the children.

'Thank you for your trouble,' said the teacher.

Jack said nothing.

'Bye-bye then,' said the ranger, and off he went.

In the barrow were eight eggs.

CHAPTER 4

The Swap

Outside the souvenir shop at the Wildlife Park there were a number of wooden tables and benches, and here at last Jack's teacher, worn down by the pleas of her class, allowed them to eat.

She divided the children up, so many to each table, and then out from holdalls or knapsacks or satchels came the lunch-boxes.

Instantly, like a large brood of nestling chicks, every mouth gaped open, and into each went sandwiches and biscuits and apples and chocolate bars.

Jack had managed to position himself at one end, and he took out his lunch-box carefully, shielding the action with his body and then placing his holdall beside him on the bench. He began to eat a sandwich hungrily, yet hardly tasting it, so stunned was he by the excitement of what he had done.

Suddenly he heard his name called.

'Jack!' cried his teacher. 'Move along a bit. Make room for Gary beside you,' and before he could do anything, Gary, the heaviest, the greediest and the stupidest boy in the class, plumped himself down, straight on top of Jack's holdall.

25

WINDSOR PUBLIC LIBRARY

'Yow!' cried Gary, hoisting himself upright again and rubbing his fat bottom in mock agony. 'What you got in there, Jack?'

Hastily Jack grabbed his holdall and put it on the ground between his feet.

'It's a football,' he said. 'If you haven't bust it, you great lump of lard! Why don't you look what you're doing?' but Gary's mouth was already too full to answer.

Jack used his feet to examine his hidden treasure as best he could. It still felt egg-shaped.

It still felt egg-shaped when they boarded the coach to return to school, and by then it had needed to survive another assault.

After the class had finished lunch, the teacher allowed the children to run around in a special play area before completing the tour of the Wildlife Park.

'Wish we had a football!' shouted one of the boys.

Gary, still eating, called out 'Jack's got one!' and he threw Jack's holdall on to the grass.

'No!' cried Jack, but before he could rescue the holdall someone took an almighty kick at it and then fell to the ground, clutching his foot.

'It'sh a hard one, innit!' said Gary with his mouth full. He sounded quite proud.

But it was nothing to Jack's pride when, at the end of the day, safely back in his bedroom at the farm, he opened the holdall and took out the ostrich egg.

Breathlessly he examined every inch of its smooth yellowish surface, but there was no sign of a crack or

blemish of any kind upon that shell that would support the weight of a twenty-stone man.

The outside of the giant egg was perfect. And just think what would come out of the inside when that shell was finally broken!

All he had to do was to wait until Lydia had laid her full clutch of eggs and was starting to sit, and then he would slip his beautiful monster under her.

At that precise moment, as Jack was imagining the warmth beneath a broody goose, a thought struck him that made his blood run cold. What if the incubation period for ostrich eggs was different from that for goose eggs?

The hatching time varied according to the kind of bird, as he well knew from his own experience. Seventeen to eighteen days for a budgerigar egg, twenty-one for a bantam's or any hen's egg, twenty-eight days for a duck egg, and for a goose egg thirty days. But what for an ostrich egg?

Quickly Jack reached down from a bookshelf his well-thumbed copy of *Birds of the World*, and scanned the index.

'. . . Orange-bird . . . Oriole . . . Ortolan . . . Osprey . . . Ostrich.'

He turned to the right page.

There were all the facts, just as the notice in the Wildlife Park had said, but how long . . .? Ah, there it was!

'. . . Incubation period – five to six weeks.'

Five to six weeks! From thirty-five to forty-two

days! But at thirty days Lydia's goslings would hatch, and Lydia would lead them out of the shed, and she and Wilfred would proudly parade around the orchard, showing off their children.

But in the deserted nest, growing colder by the moment, would lie the ostrich egg, perhaps a week or more short of hatching, and inside it, almost fully formed, an ostrich chick destined to die.

'No! No!' cried Jack out loud, cuddling his prize and stroking it as though the tiny germ of life inside it had already begun to develop. (It never occurred to him that the egg might possibly be infertile.)

'No, you *shall* hatch, I promise you! I can always breed from Lydia and Wilfred another time, but this is my only chance ever to have an ostrich of my very own.'

He sat, thinking of the great cock bird that had stared down at him that morning, and imagining his own ostrich looking just like that in a year or two's time.

(It never occurred to him that the embryo might possibly be female.)

'I shall call you Oliver,' said Jack Daw to his egg, and hiding it for the moment under his bed, went downstairs and out to see to all his birds.

When he had attended to his budgies, his bantams and his ducks, he went out into the orchard to see the geese. The four old grey ones raised their heads briefly in greeting and then went on with their grazing, but Lydia and Wilfred came running, beating their white wings and cackling loudly with pleasure. They had long ago learned that Jack kept corn in his pockets, and they nuzzled at him until he fed them.

'Have you laid a second egg, Lydia?' asked Jack, and when the white goose gave a loud honk, he said, 'Is that a Yes or a No?'

It was a Yes, he found, when he looked in the nest in the old shed under the apple tree. And every day for the next week, Lydia laid an egg, until there were nine.

Jack watched her like a hawk.

He had racked his brains to think how he could have the best of both worlds, so that when Lydia went broody, he could fix it for her to hatch both her own egg and the ostrich's, but he did not see how it could be done.

If the difference in the incubation periods had been a definite one – thirty days for a goose and thirty-five for an ostrich – he could have removed all of Lydia's as soon as she began to sit, substituted the giant one, and then put the goose eggs back under her five days later. But there was a chance, he knew, that the ostrich egg might take as long as forty-two days, so still the goslings might be out a week too early. There was only one way to ensure the birth of Oliver. All the goose eggs must go.

But Jack was not a farmer's son for nothing. A sitting of fertile goose eggs was worth a bit. Nor was he the only farmer's child in his school and he soon struck a bargain. When, on a Saturday morning, Lydia laid the last of her clutch, she little knew that at the other end of the village a couple of broody hens were ready to receive them.

Each morning Jack had gone early to the shed and found Lydia off the nest, and in it one more egg. Now, on the Saturday, she did not get off. She sat tight, looking proud and smug, and allowed Jack, the boy who had a way with birds, to stroke and fondle her, talking to her with honeyed words, while with his other hand he drew, one by one, eight eggs from beneath her and placed them carefully in a large basket. Then he took from the basket a great yellowish object and gently slid it under the sitting bird in place of the ninth and last egg.

'There!' said Jack. 'The golden egg that the goose didn't lay!' He got to his feet and stood, holding the basket and watching, his heart hammering. Now was the moment for everything to go wrong.

All right, birds could not count, but surely this one would realize that she had been duped, that one egg for nine was not fair exchange but robbery. Now she would forsake the nest and walk away and his plan would be in ruins.

But with a noise curiously like a sigh of content, and a look of great happiness, Lydia settled herself yet more deeply into the warm downy nest to begin the long incubation of what was to be, for her, a cuckoo child.

CHAPTER 5

'Ol–i–ver!'

For the first twenty-four hours, Lydia sat without moving. On the Sunday morning the boy came as usual to let them out of the old shed that kept the geese safe from the night-time fox and, when he had gone, Lydia said, 'I must leave the shed.'

'Whatever for?' said Wilfred.

As ganders go, he was a handsome fellow, but he was not blessed with a lot of brains.

'I need to go outside,' said Lydia.

'Why?' said Wilfred.

'Wilfred,' said Lydia in a patient voice, 'you surely do not wish me to foul my nest?'

'Oh!' said Wilfred. 'Oh, I see! You mean, you want to . . .?'

'Exactly,' said Lydia. 'I shall not be long. Guard the eggs,' and she stood stiffly up and waddled out into the orchard.

'Guard the eggs!' said Wilfred to himself. 'I should jolly well think I will! Why, those eggs are precious, those eggs are priceless, those eggs contain my unborn children! Woe betide anyone who threatens those eggs!' and he walked over and peered proudly into the nest.

Jack had been right – most birds are not too clever at counting, and Wilfred was much less clever than most birds. But even he was a trifle surprised to see that, instead of 'those eggs', the nest contained only one egg, an egg that appeared, even to Wilfred, to be rather on the large side.

He was still staring at it in a vacant sort of way when Lydia reappeared, comfortable now and refreshed from a quick drink and a wash-and-brush-up in the duckpond, and proceeded to tuck into the mash that the boy had left in the feeding-trough.

Wilfred cleared his throat. It would be too strong to say that he was a goose-pecked husband, but he had learned that his wife could be quite sharp with him if he failed to understand such instructions as she might give him.

'Lydia, my dear,' he said hesitantly.

'What is it?' said Lydia with her beak full.

'You did say "Guard the egg*s*"?'

'I did.'

'Well, I don't get it.'

'I should have thought,' said Lydia, 'that it would have been gosling's play to understand my remark. What is it that confuses you?'

'Look,' said Wilfred.

Lydia looked.

The moment she focused on the giant egg that was the sole occupant of her nest, Lydia reacted in two ways. First, she was surprised. Her arithmetic was not strong (except by comparison with Wilfred's) but she clearly remembered laying a number of eggs. And second, she was determined not to be shown to be in the wrong. That would never do. She thought quickly and devised a way out of the problem.

'You see,' said Wilfred, 'there's only one egg, but you said "Guard the egg*s*".'

'You misheard me, dear,' said Lydia in an affectionate tone of voice. 'What I said was "Guard the egg, sir". A respectful way, surely, to address my lord and master?'

'Oh!' said Wilfred. 'Oh yes indeed!' and he walked out into the orchard, happily hissing 'Sir! Sir! Sir!' to himself.

Lydia's third reaction, as she surveyed the huge object, was a purely instinctive one. No matter that she did not properly understand what had happened, or how or why the number of eggs that she thought she had been sitting upon had somehow magically fused into a single giant one. No need to worry your head about all that, her instincts told her – just get back on the nest and devote yourself, no matter how long it takes, to brooding this, surely the largest goose egg ever laid, out of which there must emerge the largest goose ever known.

Of all the geese in the world, she, Lydia, wife of Wilfred, had been chosen to be the mother of this marvel. Infinitely carefully, the twenty-pound bird settled herself upon the egg that would have borne a twenty-stone man.

Day followed day and week succeeded week, and Lydia sat tight in the old shed under the apple tree. Twice each day she came off the nest for a short break, while Wilfred stood on guard.

Wilfred stood on guard all day, in fact. He had become used to the size of the egg by now, having nothing to compare it with, and might well have become bored with the whole procedure had not Lydia insisted on his constant presence at her side.

'Your place is here by me,' she said, 'so you needn't think you can go gallivanting off with those old grey geese. I am doing all the work. The least you can do is to see that I am not disturbed.'

So Wilfred did sentry-go at the entrance to the shed, and ran furiously with outstretched neck and angry hissings at any hen or duck or turkey that ventured near. He even went for the farm dogs, and would no doubt have done the same to a daytime fox should one have come. But luckily, this did not happen and Lydia escaped an early widowhood. As for the humans, Wilfred would not permit Farmer Daw or his wife or Margery (all of whom imagined Lydia to be sitting on a clutch of goose eggs) to enter.

Only Jack was allowed in, partly because he was the bringer of food, and partly because, as always, he made them both feel so safe and so special, by the touch of his hand and the sound of his voice.

What he said meant nothing to them of course, except for their names. These, by constant repetition, he had taught them, as one would a dog. From the moment of their arrival Jack had addressed each by name, every time that he fondled or fed them.

'Wilfred, Wilfred, Wilfred,' he would say, stroking the gander's proud if somewhat empty head and, 'Lydia, Lydia, Lydia,' as he smoothed the goose's snowy back, and soon indeed they began to say their names themselves. To a stranger it might have appeared that the two white geese rushing to greet the boy were merely shrieking or cackling, but to Jack it was plain that one was calling 'Wilfred!' the other 'Lydia!'

Now, in the old shed under the apple tree, they learned a third name.

Morning and evening, when he came to feed them, Jack would repeat it over and over again, as one would to a parrot. To Wilfred, while Lydia was off exercising, he would say, pointing to the giant egg, 'Oliver, Oliver, Oliver.' At the same time he would turn it on to a different side, to prevent the embryo within from sticking to the shell membrane, just in case Lydia was not able to perform this instinctive task herself on so heavy an object. Then, when she came back, he would repeat the new name to her, and it was not long before they had it off by heart.

The slow learner Wilfred indeed took great pride in this new trick, and one day Farmer Daw said to his son, 'Funny thing, you know, Jack. If you listen carefully to that noisy white gander of yours, you could swear he was saying the name "Oliver". Listen!'

'I think you're right, Dad,' said Jack. 'Funny, isn't it?'

And so for forty days and forty nights Lydia bestrode her colossus. Then, very early on the morning of the forty-first day, a Thursday, she felt a movement beneath her. The very smallest of movements it was, but when she stood clear and bent her head to look, she could see that there was the very smallest of holes in the thick yellowish shell. Even as she watched, it grew larger, and within it she could see the tip of a beak. A big beak it looked too, and so it should, thought Lydia, for am I not to be the mother of the largest goose ever known!

Jack was awake early too that morning, and as

usual the first thing that caught his eye was the calendar hanging by his bed. Forty days on it were crossed off, and now surely, he thought anxiously, the ostrich egg must soon hatch. Forty-two days was the maximum incubation period and this was the forty-first, a Thursday. 'Thursday's child has far to go' said the old rhyme, but for Lydia and Wilfred, thought Jack, Thursday's child had far to grow. If only it hatched safely.

Hastily he began to dress, but even as he stood swaying, one leg in his trousers, one out, he heard from the shed in the orchard a loud cacophony of wild excited sounds.

'Ol–i–ver!' yelled Lydia and Wilfred at the tops of their voices. 'Ol–i–ver! Ol–i–ver!'

CHAPTER 6

The Duckpond

Quite what Jack expected to find when he opened the door of the shed he could never afterwards remember. As he dashed towards the orchard, his feet jammed into the wrong boots in his haste, the hubbub continued unabated.

What had happened? What were they saying? Were those cries for help, because the chick could not break free of the shell? Or were they of horror, at the sight of a child so different? Or were they, as he greatly hoped, of pure joy at a happy hatching?

What would he find in the nest? Would the great egg still be whole, cold by now, a coffin containing the body of a chick that had not had the strength to hatch? Or were the geese shouting encouragement as the baby battled its way into the world? Or had it won the fight, was it even now lying in the ruins of the egg, bedraggled, exhausted, but alive?

What Jack certainly did not expect to see was the scene that greeted him as he flung open the door.

There, standing proudly to attention like soldiers on parade, were three figures. On the right of the line stood the white gander, on the left the white goose, and between them, upright, bright-eyed and alert, stood the ostrich chick. So self-assured did he look that it was difficult to believe he had not been around for ages. Only a fragment of eggshell still sticking to his back betrayed his new-hatched status.

'Look at you!' said Jack softly.

Usually, at the sound of his voice, the geese would shout their own names in reply, but now Lydia and Wilfred bent their heads and with their beaks gently touched the top of the chick's head. Then, with one voice, they softly murmured 'Ol–i–ver', and, the introduction completed, father, mother and cuckoo child marched smartly out into the morning sunshine. Jack watched them, grinning.

'Oh Lydia! Oh Wilfred!' he said. 'If you only knew!'

But of course they didn't. They hadn't a clue.

As they walked beside their first-born, the emotion that filled the white breasts of Lydia and Wilfred was pride. Other geese might hatch out any number of ordinary common-or-garden goslings. No other geese had such a son as this! Slyly, as they grazed, they watched from the corner of their eyes this wonder child, already pecking at the flowering grass-heads, and marvelled at how different he was.

His plumage, for example, was not soft and downy and yellow, but the feathers were spiky, and striped, orange and black, and the sides of his face and his long neck were spotted with round reddish-brown dots like giant freckles. And his legs! How long and strong they already were, with the strangest feet; not for him mere webs, oh no, each of his feet bore two strong toes, and how swiftly he scampered away on them in pursuit of a passing butterfly that had caught his eye, a large brown eye brimming, the geese were sure, with intelligence of the highest order.

But to neither of them did it occur for one moment that Oliver was not of their own kind. To be sure he was unique, he was not as other goslings are, but in the course of time he would grow into the finest goose the world had ever seen. Or rather, the finest gander, for Lydia and Wilfred, no less than Jack, were convinced that they had produced a son.

Now, as they paraded him around the orchard, all the other poultry came hurrying to inspect the new arrival. The four old grey geese, the hens, the ducks, the turkeys, all looked long and hard at Oliver and then they looked at one another. No one said anything, for no one wished to provoke Wilfred into one of his rages, but the old turkey cock gave a low gobble that sounded suspiciously like laughter. Then they all went away, and, once out of earshot, cackled and clucked and quacked and gobbled at one another nineteen to the dozen with amazement and amusement.

'You see!' said Lydia proudly. 'They couldn't take their eyes off him!'

'I am not surprised,' said Wilfred. 'He is so handsome.'

'Like his father,' said Lydia.

Wilfred inclined his head in a pleased manner, but then a rare thought struck him.

'He does not much resemble me,' he said. 'His colour, those legs, the feet. Perhaps he takes after your side of the family, Lydia?'

Before Lydia could answer, a magpie landed on the grass before them and, bouncing up towards them in a jaunty way, began to hop around, head on one side, bright eyes examining every detail of the ostrich chick.

'Cor lumme luvaduck!' said the magpie loudly.

'No,' said Wilfred, 'he's a goose.'

'You could have fooled me, cock,' said the magpie.

'No,' said Wilfred, 'I'm a gander.'

'Blimey, missus,' said the magpie to Lydia, 'you've got a proper Charlie there.'

'My husband's name,' said Lydia severely, 'is Wilfred.'

'Stone the crows!' said the magpie.

It hopped closer to Oliver and stood directly in front of him, flirting its long tail up and down.

'What about you, young 'un?' it said. 'What do they call you?'

The ostrich chick did not reply. He looked uncertainly up at the geese.

'My son,' said Lydia, 'is called Oliver. If it is any business of yours. Wilfred, see this impudent bird off!'

'See it off where, dear?' said Wilfred.

'Get rid of it! Attack it! Drive it away!'

The magpie easily avoided Wilfred's clumsy charge and flitted up into an apple tree.

'Oliver! Oliver!' it squawked mockingly. 'Ask 'em what sort of bird you are, Oliver!' and it flew away, chattering with merriment.

'What did it mean, Mama?' said Oliver. 'You and me and Papa – we're all the same sort of bird, aren't we?'

'Yes, dear.'

'What sort?'

'Geese,' said Lydia.

'I'm a geese and you're a geese and Papa's a geese?'

'You can't say "a geese",' said Lydia. 'Geese means more than one goose. I'm a goose.'

'So we're three gooses? But Papa told that bird he was a gander?'

'So he is, dear. So are you, a little one.'

'But Papa said I was a goose,' said Oliver.

'You're a gosling, my lad, and little goslings should be seen and not heard, so shut your beak for a bit,' said Wilfred, and he set off for the duckpond, Lydia following.

His brow wrinkled in a frown of puzzlement, the ostrich chick ran to catch them up, and when they stopped on the rim of the pond and bent their necks for a drink, he copied them.

When they had finished and the surface of the water was once again calm, Oliver looked down and saw in its mirror three more birds. Two of them were obviously the same kind as Mama and Papa, in fact they looked very like them. But the third and smallest bird was a really weird-looking creature with spiky orange-and-black striped feathers, standing on long two-toed feet, the sides of its face and its long neck spotted with round reddish-brown dots like giant freckles.

'What an object!' thought Oliver, but at that moment all three birds disappeared as Lydia and Wilfred launched themselves into the pond and swam away.

Out in the middle they looked back to see Oliver still standing on the rim.

'Come on in, lad, the water's lovely!' shouted Wilfred, and 'Come along, Oliver, dear!' called Lydia.

Gingerly, Oliver dipped two toes in and hastily took them out again.

'It's wet,' he said.

'You're wet!' shouted Wilfred. 'Come on, lad, get in!'

'Swimming's easy, dear,' called Lydia. 'You'll see.'

Still Oliver hesitated, but the duckpond was a large one, and already Mama and Papa seemed a frighteningly long way away, so he shut his eyes and jumped off the rim.

Immediately he found himself in water so deep that only by stretching his neck to its fullest extent could he keep his head out, and a couple of frantic panic-stricken strides were enough to take that under too.

'Good lad!' shouted Wilfred from the centre of the pond, and, paddling one web only to swing himself to face his wife, he said, "The lad's got spirit after all! For a first dive, that wasn't half bad!' Lydia did not reply, but only watched the surface.

'He hasn't come up again,' she said.

CHAPTER 7

Sooner or Later

Jack had stood outside the shed under the apple tree, watching everything that went on in the orchard. He saw Oliver introduced to the rest of the flock of poultry. He saw the magpie fly down and Wilfred drive it away. He saw the family walk towards the duckpond, and not a hint of possible danger crossed his mind, so full was it of other thoughts.

At first, these were all of joy and excitement that he was now the proud owner of a fine specimen of *Struthio camelus*, the Camel Bird, the largest feathered creature in all the world. Oliver was his!

But even as he said this to himself, he was struck by a much less comfortable thought. The fact that he had taken the egg from the ranger's barrow had not worried him one bit during all the weeks of its incubation. It would only have been fed to a python. He had saved it from that. That had to be a good thing. But suddenly, as he watched a real live ostrich chick running about in the orchard, he realized that, strictly, Oliver was not his. Oliver belonged to the Wildlife Park. Oliver had been stolen. He was a thief. That had to be a bad thing.

What would the people at the Wildlife Park say if they knew?

What would his father say when he knew?

Would he make him take Oliver back?

Suddenly all these thoughts were shattered by a wild scream from Lydia, and Jack, looking up, saw to his horror that Oliver was no longer standing by the rim of the duckpond. There was no sign of him. By the time Jack reached the pond, bubbles were beginning to rise to the surface.

They say that, when you are drowning, all of your past life flashes before your eyes. If that is so, very old people must take a long time to drown, but though Oliver's past life spanned no more than a quarter of an hour, he was pretty waterlogged by the time Jack hoicked him out. To all intents and purposes, he looked dead.

Jack had learned about First Aid in swimming classes at school, but he wasn't too sure about mouth-to-beak resuscitation, and as for thumping the chick's little chest, that would finish him off if he wasn't already gone.

In fact, and by chance, Jack did the right thing.

First, he sought help. Second, as he ran at top speed for the farmhouse, he carried the chick upside down in one hand, holding it by its legs, its long neck dangling like a bell-pull and swinging and jerking about.

So that by the time he reached the kitchen where his mother was preparing breakfast, a lot of the water in Oliver's lungs had drained out.

'Mum! Mum!' shrieked Jack, laying the ostrich chick on the kitchen table. 'He fell in the duckpond! I think he's drowned!'

Like all farmers' wives, Mrs Daw was used to dealing with animal emergencies. She did not waste time asking questions but picked up the chick and felt its bedraggled body.

'His heart's beating,' she said, 'but he's cold and shocked,' and quickly she wrapped him in a towel. Only his head stuck out, the eyes closed, but as they watched, Oliver gave a feeble splutter. Then he sicked up some more pond water.

'He'll do,' said Jack's mother. 'Funny thing, but it takes a long time for young creatures to drown. That's why it's so cruel when people drown kittens. Now then, into the Aga with him. Open the door of the bottom oven, Jack,' and when Jack did so, she put the wrapped chick on the lowest shelf.

'Watch him,' she said. 'I must get on with the breakfast.'

Jack knelt by the open oven door, praying for Oliver to open his eyes, and in a minute or so, he did. Already, Jack noticed, he had lovely long eyclashes. Then he made a funny little sound, part cheep, part croak, part belch. To anyone else it would have been just a noise. To Jack, who had a way with birds, it was no problem to translate.

Oliver was saying, 'Thank you.'

By the time that Jack's father had come hungrily in from his cowshed, and Jack's sister Margery had come sleepily down from her bedroom, for breakfast, Oliver was restored to health. Ten minutes in the low oven, then a gentle towelling from Jack, and finally, from Jack's mother, a small teaspoonful of cooking sherry, had made a new chick of him, and he was walking, albeit a trifle shakily, about the kitchen floor.

'Do we have to have one of Jack's beastly birds running about when we're eating?' grumbled Margery.

'He fell in the duckpond,' said her mother. 'We've just been drying him out.'

'He's called Oliver,' said Jack.

Jack's father picked up the chick in his large farmer's hands.

'So you've been a taking a bath, Oliver?' he said.

'Doesn't look to me as though you're any kind of waterfowl, not with feet like that.'

He examined one of Oliver's strange two-toed feet, and looked at the length of his legs and of his neck, and at his odd freckled markings. Then he gave him to Jack to hold.

'I've seen a few chicks of one sort or another in my time,' said Farmer Daw, 'but never one like this fellow.'

'I haven't asked you, Jack,' said Mrs Daw, 'because I knew your father would. But now I think you'd better tell us. What is it?'

Gently Jack stroked Oliver's back, dry and warm again now.

'It's an ostrich,' he said.

'An ostrich?' cried Margery. 'Oh you are a little liar, Jack!'

'I'm not,' said Jack. 'I got an ostrich egg from the Wildlife Park when my class went on that trip, and I set it under Lydia, and she hatched it out, this morning.'

'Wait a minute,' said his father. 'You say you got an ostrich egg. How did you get it?'

'Were you given it?' asked his mother.

'No.'

'Did you buy it?' asked his father.

'No.'

'You stole it!' cried Margery. 'Oh you are a little thief, Jack! You stole it, didn't you?'

'Yes,' said Jack. 'I did.'

'Eat your breakfast, both of you,' said his mother to her husband and her daughter, and to her son she said, 'You'd better tell us all about it.'

So Jack told them the whole story, from the moment when he had first set eyes on the magnificent black-and-white bird, half as tall again as a man, one of whose sons he now held in his arms.

When he had finished there was a moment's silence.

Then, 'You'll have to take him back,' said Farmer Daw.

'Oh Dad,' said Jack quietly. 'Not yet?'

''Course you will,' said Margery. 'He doesn't belong to you. He belongs to the Wildlife Park. You pinched him.'

'I didn't pinch *him*,' said Jack. 'I pinched an egg, that was going to be fed to a snake. Nobody wanted it. It might not even have been fertile for all I knew. If it hadn't been for me, Oliver wouldn't have been born, and if it hadn't been for me, he'd have been drowned by now,' and he hugged the ostrich chick to him, blinking away the threat of tears.

Margery opened her mouth for a further taunt, but her mother silenced her with a fierce frown and a shake of the head. She caught her husband's eye and made, to him, a quite different face, eyebrows raised, head a little on one side, with the hint of a smile.

Farmer Daw swallowed his last mouthful and pushed his chair back from the table.

'We shall have to think about this, Jack,' he said.

'Stealing is stealing, however you dress it up. And anyway, fancy having an ostrich on the farm! Whoever heard of such a thing!' He grinned, despite himself.

'He'll have to go back,' he said. 'Sooner or later.'

'Later, Dad,' said Jack. 'Please!'

His father hesitated in the kitchen doorway. Through the opened door they could all hear a doleful duet coming from the orchard.

'Ol–i–ver! Ol–i–ver!' cried Lydia and Wilfred, in mourning, as they thought, for their lost child.

'Oh go on then,' said Farmer Daw. 'Put him back with them. But only for the time being, mind.'

'Yes, Dad! Thanks, Dad!' said Jack, and he ran for the orchard, carrying Oliver, this time the right way up.

CHAPTER 8

The Most Marvellous Goose

'Oliver darling!' cried Lydia. 'Oh my poor baby! Are you all right?'

'Yes, thank you, Mama,' said Oliver.

'Oh I shall never forget it as long as I live!' said Lydia. 'That terrible moment when you didn't come up again! It was the mud, I suppose, you got your feet stuck in the mud, that must have been it, nasty sticky stuff, it's those dirty ducks, they make it so mucky, you mustn't go in that pond again till you're much bigger.'

'No, Mama,' said Oliver. 'I won't.'

'There's a good gosling,' said Lydia. 'Oh Oliver, I can't tell you what it's been like! We've been out of our minds with worry, your father and I, haven't we, Wilfred?'

Wilfred did not answer.

Truth to tell, he had not been out of such little mind as he had with worry, not for long, for by now it had become filled with a mixture of disappointment and scorn. Coming as he did from a proud line of waterfowl, for whom swimming was as natural as walking (and more gracefully performed at that), he found it very hard to stomach the bitter fact that a son of his had simply sunk.

Stuck in the mud – my web! he thought. The lad had panicked. Like many stupid folk, Wilfred was brave purely because he had never known the meaning of fear, and to suspect his son of being a coward was agony. But that's what he is, he said to himself. The lad's chicken! His thoughts were interrupted by the sound of his wife's voice.

'Wilfred!' she said sharply. 'I asked you a question. Well?'

Sometimes, if Wilfred had not listened to, or, more likely, had not understood Lydia's questions, he would take an even-money gamble and answer either 'Yes' or 'No'. But this could earn him a smart dressing-down if he guessed wrong, so he had devised a slightly safer method.

'I quite agree, my dear,' he said.

'You see,' said Lydia to Oliver. 'Papa was worried stiff too.'

And still is, thought Wilfred.

'Oliver, lad,' he said.

'Yes, Papa?'

'*Why* did you sink?'

'Wilfred!' cried Lydia. 'Do you listen to *nothing* I say? I told you, he got his feet stuck in the mud, didn't you, Oliver?'

'No, Mama,' said Oliver.

He turned to face the gander.

'It's quite simple, Papa,' he said. 'I sank because I cannot swim.'

There was a silence as the two geese digested this remark, in differing ways.

Wilfred felt suddenly much happier. It looked as though the lad might not be chicken after all. In fact, thought Wilfred, if he jumped in knowing he could not swim, that was a brave thing to do! (For Wilfred, 'brave' and 'foolhardy' were one and the same thing.) What it all meant was that here was a gosling who, for some as yet unexplained reason, had not learned to swim.

'Don't worry, lad!' he shouted. 'I'll soon teach you!'

'Wilfred!' said Lydia angrily. 'You heard me tell Oliver that he is not to go into that pond until he is much bigger. Perhaps you will be good enough in future not to contradict, contravene, gainsay or generally run counter to my express instructions!'

Puzzled by his wife's language but warned by the tone of her voice, Wilfred played it safe.

'I quite agree, my dear,' he said.

Lydia's reaction on hearing the ostrich chick say that he could not swim had been very different. A degree of logical thought – something denied Wilfred – was within her grasp, and it went as follows:

All geese can swim.

Oliver cannot swim.

Therefore Oliver is not a goose.

For the first time a shadow of doubt concerning

her child crossed Lydia's mind. Admittedly she had never had a gosling of her own before, but she had been one herself, not all that long ago, and she could clearly remember, thinking about it now, what her brothers and sisters had looked like. And they had not looked at all like Oliver.

So what is he? Of what, she asked herself perplexedly, am I the mother?

For an instant she considered sharing her doubts with her husband, but as quickly rejected the idea. Just supposing Oliver were not a goose, still Wilfred would always consider him one, even if he grew nine feet tall! As for me, she said to herself, I don't care. He's alive and safe and beautiful, and he's my son!

'Come along, Oliver darling,' she said. 'The boy is bringing your breakfast now. You must eat up every scrap and then you'll grow up to be big and strong. Why, who knows, one day you might even be bigger than Papa, mightn't he, Wilfred?' and Wilfred, who hadn't listened to a word, said, 'I quite agree, my dear.'

How Jack, watching, would have laughed if he could have understood Lydia's last remark. He could of course interpret a certain amount of goose speech – shouts of welcome, cries of alarm, companionable chucklings and honkings and mutterings, angry noises when Wilfred lost his temper with dog or turkey cock or Lydia lost her temper with Wilfred – and now he set himself to try to fathom the rudiments of ostrich language.

As the days passed, Jack became aware of one particular sound that Oliver made, almost constantly, as he foraged in the orchard with his foster parents. It was a shrill thin whistle. There was never any difficulty in finding where Oliver was. You could hear him whistling.

At first Jack worried about this, thinking it might be some kind of distress call, until one day he found, in the public library, a large modern reference book on birds. It had much more to say about ostriches than his old edition of *Birds of the World*, and it explained the noise.

'Often,' it said, 'a number of broods of ostrich chicks of much the same age will band together in one flock, of as many as forty or fifty individuals. Contact between these chicks, as they search for food among the tall grass, is maintained by sound, each chick keeping up a constant whistling.'

The book also described the call of the adult male ostrich, 'a hollow booming noise, used as an alarm or as a threat; this "boom" is very like the distant roar of a lion but without the terminal grunt.'

At about a month old, Oliver began to give up whistling, presumably because there was no one to whistle back at him, but by then he was making three other noises that Jack could clearly distinguish.

The first was '*Boo!*' – not the jeering sneering boo of an angry football fan but a short sudden noise such as you might make on jumping out from hiding to frighten someone.

The second was '*Twoo!*' This was a softer long-drawn-out sound, not melancholy like an owl's hoot but on a gentle happy note.

The third was '*Hrup!*' – the noise of a man clearing his throat.

'*Boo!*' Jack learned, was used as a greeting ('Hullo!' or 'Good morning!' or 'Nice to see you!') or as a summons ('Come and see what I've found, Mama' or 'Hurry up with my breakfast.')

'*Twoo!*' meant happiness, pleasure at being stroked and petted, delight at finding a fat worm, or the simple joy of running about in the sunshine on ever-lengthening legs.

The meaning of '*Hrup!*' was made plain to Jack one morning when he had scattered a handful of chick crumbs on the grass for Oliver. This was a useful way of feeding the ostrich chick, for Lydia and Wilfred were clumsy at picking up these crumbs, allowing Oliver the lion's share. But, as Jack watched, one of his bantam hens came running up to steal food from under the ostrich's very beak.

'*Hrup!*' said Oliver loudly, and he gave the little bird a hefty kick that sent it scuttling away in squawking fright.

And so the weeks passed, and with them Jack's fear grew. For how much longer would he be allowed to keep his unusual pet?

'He'll have to go back,' Father had said. 'Sooner or later.'

How soon was 'later'?

Jack's fear was, however, not the only thing that was growing. So also was his family's affection for the ostrich chick.

To the farmer, the sight of a healthy thriving animal of any sort was a pleasure, and this exotic creature particularly took his fancy.

Mrs Daw, perhaps because of her part in the rescue from the duckpond, perhaps from a fellow feeling with Lydia's obvious maternal pride, found that she had a very soft spot for Jack's pet.

And even Margery, who normally took no notice of any of her brother's birds, had (though she would never have admitted it to Jack) come under Oliver's spell: he had come running to her one day as she crossed the orchard and had serenaded her with so warm and full-throated a '*Twoo!*' that she quite fell for him.

Fastest growing of all, of course, was not Jack's worry or the family's liking, but Oliver himself.

At birth he had been a foot tall. Now, at six months of age, he was three times that height, towering over Lydia and Wilfred. And how, indeed, they looked up to him!

Lydia, though she did not know (and would never know) what he was, knew without doubt that her amazing child was the most marvellous creature. Wilfred thought him the most marvellous goose.

He had accepted the fact that Oliver could not swim or (so far as he knew) fly. But what filled him with pride was the speed of the lad! At about four weeks old, Oliver had begun to run really fast, startling the old grey geese and the hens and the ducks and the turkeys as he flashed by them. But now he had shifted into top gear.

'The ostrich is capable of speeds of between 30 and 40 m.p.h.,' said the bird book, and for slowcoach Wilfred it was sheer delight to watch his sprinting son.

'Look at him!' he shouted at Lydia one morning as Oliver hurtled by with the speed of a galloping horse. 'There's never been a goose like that!' and Lydia, with a wry cackle, replied, 'I quite agree, my dear.'

Jack and his father were watching too.

'Look at him!' said Farmer Daw. 'However much bigger is he going to grow?'

'It says in the books, four foot high at one year of age, and eight foot or more when fully grown,' said Jack. 'Nine foot, some are.'

'Nine foot! That's half as tall again as me! He won't fit in that shed under the apple tree then.'

Jack swallowed.

'He won't be here then, Dad, will he?'

'Well no, I suppose not.'

'You said he'll have to go back, to the Wildlife Park.'

'Well, yes.'

'When?'

At that moment Oliver drew up before them, scarcely out of breath. He stared at them with his large brown eyes and fluttered his long long lashes.

'*Boo!*' he said politely, and, stretching out his serpentine neck, offered to each in turn the top of his head for a scratch, something he particularly enjoyed.

'*Twoo!*' said Oliver softly to the father, and '*Twoo!*' again to the son.

Jack sighed deeply.

'Dad,' he said, 'when *will* he have to go back?'

Farmer Daw grinned a trifle sheepishly.

'Oh, sooner or later,' he said.

CHAPTER 9

'I only wanted to play!'

On his first birthday, Oliver hit the roof.

For some time now he had towered above his foster parents, but that morning when Jack opened the door of the old shed under the apple tree, he saw that the top of Oliver's head was actually touching the tin roof.

'Happy birthday, dear Oliver, happy birthday to you!' sang Jack, a trifle sadly and then he added, 'for I don't suppose I'll sing it again next year – you'll be gone.'

He fed the family and then he went and borrowed a rule from his father's workshop, and measured the inside height of the shed. Four feet – just as the books had said.

Jack folded the rule, and was just about to go out when he saw, in the darkest corner of the shed, a nest, and, in it, a goose egg!

Before very many days had passed, Lydia completed her clutch and was sitting, and a month after that, she hatched eight goslings.

How thrilled everyone was, when first she marched them out into the orchard! Jack was delighted, it goes without saying. Wilfred was bursting with fatherly pride. And how excited Oliver was!

When Lydia first began to sit, he had been puzzled.

'Aren't you coming out with us, Mama?' he said, bending his long neck and fluttering his long eyelashes at her.

'No, dear,' said Lydia. 'I'm just going to sit here for a while.'

Oliver ran to find Wilfred.

'*Boo!*' he said, and then, as he strode beside the gander very slowly, to keep pace, 'Papa. What's the matter with Mama?'

'Matter?' said Wilfred. 'Nothing's the matter, lad. You'll soon have lots of brothers and sisters. Your mother's going to have a lot of babies, that's what she's going to do.'

'Oh,' said Oliver. He had forgotten his own birth and he was vague about the whole business.

'Baby whats?' he said.

'Baby goslings of course.'

'Like me?'

Wilfred raised his head from the grass and looked up at the young ostrich. For some months now he had taken Oliver rather for granted, not really noticing the changes in him. Now he stared up and saw a four-foot high young giant, quite different in colouring; gone were the reddish-brown dots from face and neck, and the spiky orange-and-black striped feathers had softened and darkened, except for wing and tail plumes, which were white. How long his neck is too, thought Wilfred, and his legs, how muscular they are, and his glance, travelling downwards, fell upon those huge two-toed feet.

'She's going to have goslings like me?' asked Oliver again.

Wilfred shook his head violently, as though to clear his thoughts.

'No,' he said. 'They will not be like you are now, because you have grown big. You are not a gosling any more.'

'What am I then?'

'You are a gander,' said Wilfred. 'Like me.'

They walked forward to the rim of that pond that, thirteen months ago, had nearly been the death of Oliver, and stood, looking down at their reflections in the water.

'Like you?' said Oliver doubtfully.

But he forgot his doubts when first he saw his eight little brothers and sisters. He could only think how pretty they were, as they toddled along in Indian file behind Lydia.

'*Twoo! Twoo!*' he cried, and he cantered towards them, eager for a game with these new playmates.

Mercifully he did not step on any of them, but several were tipped over by the ostrich's huge feet, and lay helplessly on their backs, paddling their little webs in the air and peeping with fright.

Furious at his clumsiness, Lydia flew at him, buffeting him with her wings, and, as he turned away, an equally angry Wilfred came hissing at him and biting at his legs.

'Mama! Papa!' cried Oliver in distress. 'I only wanted to play!' but the two white geese were already hustling the goslings away. Straight for the duckpond they made, and as Oliver watched, the memory of his own first (and almost last) day of life flashed into his horrified mind. If there had been sand about, perhaps he would have buried his head in it, but as it was, he could only shut his eyes. But when at last he opened them again, it was to see the eight goslings swimming easily and happily about with their parents.

Jack, who had been watching all this, now came up and put an arm round his long neck.

'Poor Oliver!' he said. 'It's hard for you to understand, isn't it?'

'*Hrup!*' said Oliver, not in anger but in sorrow. He turned his head at right angles, a trick he had, to look directly at Jack, and his great brown eyes, the boy could see, were full of sadness.

'I'm afraid you're just going to have to get used to it,' said Jack. 'Lydia and Wilfred are bound to be pretty wrapped up in these new babies. You're going to have to take a back seat. But you're my favourite, you know that, don't you?'

He scratched the top of the ostrich's head, now almost level with his own, and Oliver managed a faint '*Twoo*'.

'Just be careful where you're putting your big feet,' said Jack.

'Just be careful where you're putting your big feet,' said Wilfred sharply when he and Lydia returned with the goslings.

'Yes, Papa,' said Oliver.

Lydia, seeing him look so woebegone, spoke in kinder tones.

'Better still, don't move till we're safely past you, Oliver dear, there's a good goose,' she said.

'Yes, Mama,' said Oliver.

He stood motionless until the file of goslings began to pass him, but then he couldn't resist stretching his neck down until his head was on a level with theirs.

'Awfully sorry I knocked you over,' he said, as quietly as he could, but the goslings all stampeded wildly, peeping with fright.

Worse was to follow.

At twilight the white geese and their eight new children made for the safety and shelter of the old shed, but Oliver, following, found his way barred. Wilfred stood in the entrance.

'Sorry, lad,' he said gruffly. 'You'll have to doss down somewhere else. Your mother's frightened you'll tread on the goslings, and the goslings are frightened of you. You're too big.'

At that moment Jack arrived on his evening rounds, shutting up all the different sorts of poultry in all the different sheds and houses to be safe from the fox.

He saw at once what was happening.

'Inside, Wilfred,' he said, and Wilfred obeyed,

and Jack shut the door. 'Come along, Oliver,' he said. 'We'll find you a place of your very own, and get you something special for supper.'

The place turned out to be an old stable, where horses had lived in the days before tractors, and where there was plenty of space and headroom. The supper was a large apple.

As a little chick, Oliver had pecked and swallowed – at grass, beetles, worms, woodlice, at anything edible. Each bit of food went straight down, But now, nearly adult, he had begun to eat as grown-up ostriches do, retaining food in his mouth until there was enough to form quite a large ball or bolus, which he would then swallow, so that a watcher could see the spherical shape travelling slowly down the long throat.

Jack stood a moment, watching the apple descend like a plumb bob, and then, after a final scratch on the top of Oliver's head, he bolted the stable door.

Oliver got little sleep that night. For hours, he padded up and down the length of the cobbled stable floor, feeling extremely sorry for himself. True, the boy had been, as always, nice to him, but Mama and Papa had not only attacked him but turned him away, from his home, from his birthplace. 'It's not fair!' said Oliver. '*Hrup!* It's jolly well not fair!' and in his frustration he kicked out with one of his sharp-clawed two-toed feet at a bucket that stood on the floor and sent it spinning across the stable. At last, tired out, he folded his long legs beneath him and sank to the floor, neck outstretched and chin resting on the cobbles, and slept.

Oliver got to his feet when Jack came to let him out but his spirits did not rise. Lydia and Wilfred took only the barest notice of his greeting '*Boo!*', so preoccupied were they with the goslings, and would shout a warning 'Ol–i–ver!' each time he approached too closely.

Jack, watching, worried. Just why a stout bucket in the stable had two gaping holes torn in it he did not know, but he did know that Oliver was unhappy, and why.

He's been rejected by his family, he thought. But, of course, they're not really his family. He should be with his own kind. Oh, I don't want to lose him, the last thing I want is to lose him, but perhaps it's time for him to go back to the Wildlife Park.

For days Jack agonized about this, but then, when the goslings were a couple of weeks old, something happened that was to postpone any such decision.

It was a sunny Sunday morning, and though there is no day of rest for a farming family, the Daws were taking it easy. Mr and Mrs Daw were looking through the papers, Margery was reading a novel and Jack was deep in *Birds of the World*.

Out in the orchard the various poultry cackled and clucked and quacked and gobbled, enjoying the warmth and without a care in the world.

Lydia and Wilfred grazed side by side, their minds, now that their children were older, not so constantly on them. They had not noticed in fact that the eight goslings, busily hunting among the grasses for insects, had strayed towards the far end of the orchard. It was bounded here by a dry-stone wall, beyond which was a wood.

As the goslings neared the wall, they suddenly saw that, lying flat upon the top of it, was an animal. To their innocent eyes it looked something like one of the farm dogs, to which they were already accustomed, knowing they would do them no harm. To be sure, the farm dogs were black-and-white, and this little dog was a fiery russet red, but that meant nothing to the goslings. Peeping and cheeping to one another, they wandered closer. On the wall the fox lay, almost as still as a statue. The only movement it made was to lick its lips.

CHAPTER 10

'BOOM!'

The fox was an old one, and full of wisdom. A night hunter like all his kind, he was none the less a specialist in daytime raids. This one he had planned carefully.

A few days before he had slipped down from his earth in a distant hillside to have a good look at the lie of the land. Behind the buildings of the farm, he had found, there was an orchard, filled with a variety of poultry, and at the far eastern end of the orchard was a wood.

Behind the dry-stone wall at the wood's edge he had paused and tested the breeze with his sharp nose. The prevailing west wind brought him a medley of farmyard smells, many of them mouth-watering; but on that particular morning one of the farm collies had chanced to be crossing the orchard, and at the scent of it the fox had melted back into the wood.

Now, he had once again come in upwind, and this time found nothing to worry about, for the dogs were asleep at Farmer Daw's feet as he read the Sunday papers.

The old fox had lain luxuriantly on the wall-top, savouring the delicious aroma of hen and duck and goose and turkey, and watching the eight goslings draw near. Beyond them he could see poultry of every size and shape, including one bird that was unfamiliar to him as it stood by itself on ridiculously long legs.

A gosling, the fox thought, is not much more than a mouthful, but I'll pull off their silly little heads before I get myself something more substantial. One of those two white geese, for example – that'd be worth taking home. He licked his lips.

So confident was the fox of there being plenty of time to go about his butchery undisturbed that he stood up and stretched, prior to jumping down from the wall. The movement was seen by the sharpest pair of eyes in the orchard.

Oliver had been standing by himself, wanting to go and forage beside his little brothers and sisters, but not daring to for fear of a telling-off.

At least I may look at them, he thought, there can't be any harm in that, and he stared at the eight distant shapes with those great eyes whose keen sight give the ostrich, on its native African plains, early warning of any far-off enemy. What kind of animal it was that now dropped from the dry-stone wall he did not know, but it looked unusual, and interesting.

'*Boo!*' said Oliver loudly, and at the sound Lydia looked up from her grazing and saw the fox.

'Children!' she shrieked. 'Come to Mama! Run, quickly!' and the goslings, startled, scuttled to obey.

Behind them padded the self-assured raider, in no hurry, enjoying the little victims' panic, content to play cat-and-mouse with them, particularly as the two foolish white geese were now rushing directly towards him, aiming, it seemed, to run down his throat!

Wildly, Lydia and Wilfred beat their wings as they hastened, screeching, across the grass in a gallant attempt at rescue that could only have ended in death for the whole family. But while they were still fifty yards away, and when the fox was but a few feet from the hindmost of the madly fleeing goslings, a tall figure shot past the hurrying geese. Oliver might only have been half-grown but already he could run at full speed, the amazing speed of *Struthio camelus*, the Camel Bird, and as he passed Lydia and Wilfred, they might as well have been standing still. His little brothers and sisters were in mortal danger – that he knew from their panic-stricken cries and the anguished voices of his mother and father – and as he ran, there burst from him in his anger his first ever adult sound, 'a booming noise ... like the distant roar of a lion'.

'BOOM!!' bellowed Oliver as he raced to the rescue at forty miles an hour.

At the sound the old fox, his jaws already agape to fasten on the slowest gosling, hesitated for a second, but in that second one life was saved and another lost. A last bound took Oliver clean over the goslings' heads, and as he landed before the snarling fox, he lashed out with one mighty kick that sent a fiery russet red shape whirling and twirling into the air, to fall flat, and twitch twice, and lie limp.

Oliver stood beside the lifeless foe, wings and plumed tail raised, head held high, and danced a short jig of victory.

'BOOM!' he roared once more.

Then the fire died out of his great eyes, his wings dropped to his side, and he lowered his head as Lydia and Wilfred arrived upon the scene, breathless from running and from sheer amazement. Behind them trailed the eight goslings, wide-eyed with wonder; they did not understand what had been happening, but they dimly realized that this enormous brother of theirs, of whom they had all been so scared, had saved their lives. Nervously, the boldest of them made his way forward to stand by the ostrich's feet, and, tipping his little head right back, peeped a message of thanks on behalf of them all.

'*Twoo!*' said Oliver very softly, and he bent his head to the ground and gently touched beaks with the spokesperson.

Lydia and Wilfred stood side by side, looking at the dead fox.

'Oliver darling,' said Lydia, 'you were wonderful.'

'Good lad, Oliver!' said Wilfred in his heartiest voice. 'I'm proud of you, my son! A gander killing a fox! Imagine that!'

'I shouldn't, if I were you,' said Lydia drily.

She looked at those great two-toed feet, around which the goslings, their fear of their big brother gone, were happily waddling on their little webs. Once again a piece of logic occurred to her:

All geese have webbed feet.

Oliver has not got webbed feet.

Therefore Oliver is not a goose.

And thanks be that he's not, she thought. But for him we should all be dead, and many of the other birds too, I dare say. She looked down the orchard to see the old grey geese and the hens and ducks and turkeys, all of which had fled at sight of the fox, cautiously returning.

And through them now came the Daw family, at the run.

At the first 'BOOM!' Jack, who knew immediately the origin of that noise, threw down *Birds of the World* and dashed out, calling the dogs, and the others followed as the second 'BOOM!' sounded.

Now they reached the scene, breathless from running and from sheer amazement, and gazed down at the body lying in the grass, while the collies sniffed, with low growls and raised hackles, at the two gaping holes torn in its side. Jack, watching, recalled the stable bucket.

'What . . .?' began Margery.

'How . . .?' said Mrs Daw.

'Who . . .?' said Farmer Daw.

'Oliver,' said Jack. 'A kick from a full-grown ostrich can kill a man, the ranger at the Wildlife Park told us, so a kick from a half-grown one can kill a fox. Oliver has saved the goslings' lives!'

'And a lot more lives besides,' said his father. 'You know what a fox is like – as long as anything flutters in front of him, he'll kill it. There would have been a massacre here this morning but for your Oliver, Jack.'

'Oh Oliver!' said Jack. 'You're a hero!' and the ostrich replied, '*Twoo! Twoo!*'

'Sounds like he's saying "Too true"!' laughed Jack's mother. 'Ah well, time I made a start with the lunch.'

Farmer Daw looked down at the dead fox, the brightness of that red coat already seemingly faded.

'No more Sunday lunches for you, you old devil,' he said, and he picked the animal up by the brush.

'One of you children fetch a spade,' he said.

By the time Farmer Daw had finished digging a hole, most of the orchard's inhabitants had already forgotten the morning's drama, though the goslings had had to listen to a severe lecture from Lydia.

'You are never,' she had ended, 'to stray away by yourselves like that again, do you understand? Mama is very angry with you indeed!' and Wilfred, reckoning that what was sauce for the goose was sauce for the gander, added, 'And Papa is very angry too. You must do as Mama says, or you will never grow up to be big geese.'

'Like Oliver?' said one of the goslings.

Wilfred hesitated, confused, but Lydia said briskly, 'Now come along, all of you, follow me,' and off they went.

Only Oliver stood by the hole at Jack's side, watching gravely as the farmer tipped into it the body of the fox and began to shovel back the earth.

So intent was the burial party on the business that nobody noticed behind them a blue-uniformed figure entering the orchard and walking, with steps that were noiseless on the turf, towards them.

'Dad,' said Jack, as his father thumped the little mound of earth with the flat of the spade. 'We can't send him back now. Not after what he's done.'

Farmer Daw sighed.

'I don't rightly know what to do,' he said. 'Trouble is, you can't just forget how he came to be here, you know. That egg he came out of was not your property. You stole it. You may not like it, Jack, but the fact remains – you're a thief.'

'Hullo, 'ullo, 'ullo,' said a voice behind them, and man, boy and ostrich turned to see the local police sergeant.

'What's all this then, Mr Daw?' he said. 'You say your son's a thief?'

CHAPTER 11

A Lump in the Throat

'And before you answer that,' said the sergeant, 'what in the world's that thing standing by you?'

He stared quizzically at Oliver, and Oliver fluttered his eyelashes at him and uttered a quiet polite '*Boo!*'

'Fierce, is it?' said the sergeant to Jack, but before he could answer, his father said, 'No, he wouldn't say "boo" to a goose.'

This was so far from the truth – for every morning Oliver greeted his fosterparents in this fashion – that Jack had to stifle a giggle, despite the seriousness of the situation. But then his spirits fell.

It was all up now. The policeman would report him to the Director of the Wildlife Park, and Oliver would have to go back there, and he would probably go to prison for stealing the egg.

Better make a clean breast of it, now, it might count in his favour.

'Please,' he said, 'it's my ostrich, I mean it's an ostrich, and his name is Oliver, and he's saved the lives of all our poultry by killing a fox that we've just been burying here, and one of my geese hatched him out of an egg' (he paused for breath) 'that I stole from the Wildlife Park.'

The police sergeant took off his helmet and scratched the top of his head, thoughtfully.

Jack scratched the top of Oliver's, nervously.

'I don't know, I'm sure,' said the sergeant. 'I come out here to get your dad to buy a couple of raffle tickets in aid of the Police Benevolent Fund, and what do I find? A dead body, a bird that's a murderer, and a boy that's guilty of larceny. And I shouldn't be surprised if there weren't other offences to be taken into consideration. You may need a licence to keep an ostrich. And third party insurance, I shouldn't wonder. And how about the Wild Birds Protection Act? Taking the eggs of a rare bird, as I remember, carries a penalty of a fine of £25 or a month's imprisonment, for a first offence.'

Jack looked so downcast at this that the police sergeant, a kindly man, hastened to reassure him.

'I'm joking,' he said. 'Don't worry – I'm not going to say anything about your precious ostrich. That's up to your dad to sort out. I'll keep my mouth shut – on one condition.'

'What's that?' asked Jack fearfully.

'That your father buys a whole book of these here raffle tickets.'

'Thanks, sergeant,' said Farmer Daw. 'I'll certainly do that. And look, don't you worry either, we're going to put this matter right and straight – with the Wildlife Park, I mean.'

'Just as well, Mr Daw,' said the police sergeant. 'I know you're pretty isolated here, and this orchard's tucked away around the back, but sooner or later someone's going to set eyes on this fellow and then you'll have the press here and the television and the Lord knows what. Fancy having an ostrich on the farm, whoever heard of such a thing!'

'What are we going to do, Dad?' said Jack, when the policeman had gone.

'We're going to drive over to the Wildlife Park this very afternoon, you and me, and we're going to see the Director, and you're going to tell him everything. Better make a clean breast of it, now, it might count in your favour.'

Jack ate very little of that Sunday lunch. He felt sick. Owning up to something bad that you've done is always difficult, and now he must not only own up, and be punished, but lose Oliver too. One day, he had been telling himself for a long while now, Oliver would have to go, but now that day was almost here. Tomorrow, probably, they would come for him with a van or a truck and cart him off. Just when he's become a hero, thought Jack – to my family and to his.

He ran to the orchard gate while his father was getting the car out and looked over.

There were Lydia and Wilfred, paddling placidly on the pond, enjoying each other's company and free for the moment from the trials of parenthood.

The children were safe and happy, they knew, in the charge of the childminder, who was taking them for a walk.

Oliver took one slow pace to twenty of each of theirs, terribly careful where he was putting his big feet, while the eight goslings scuttered merrily about, piping and peeping at their giant brother.

Oliver looked up and saw Jack.

'*Boo!*' he said cheerily, and then returned to duty, with many a soft '*Twoo!*' to his little charges, and one loud '*Hrup!*' when the turkey cock approached too closely.

All the way to the Wildlife Park Jack tried to convince himself that the Director would be as nice as the police sergeant. The sergeant had been large and stout, and his round clean-shaven face had broken easily into a smile. He looked like a friendly bear.

But when they were admitted to the Director's office, he wasn't a bit like that. He was small and thin, with a narrow face and a ginger beard. He reminded Jack of the late fox.

'Mr . . . Daw, is it?' he said to Jack's father. 'What can I do for you?' Farmer Daw put his hand on Jack's shoulder and gave it a reassuring squeeze.

'This is my boy Jack,' he said. 'He has something to tell you.'

'Yes?' said the Director.

Jack tried hard to keep his voice steady but all the same it trembled as he said, 'I stole one of your ostrich eggs.'

Slowly, the Director put up a paw and pulled at his ginger beard. His face wore so foxy a look that Jack began to feel like a helpless gosling.

'How?' said the Director softly.

'It was last year,' said Jack. 'I came here with a party from my school. The ranger was showing us some ostrich eggs – spare ones, that he was going to feed to the snakes – and I pinched one.'

'You are an egg collector,' said the Director, and there was a snarl in his voice.

'No!' said Jack. 'No, I think taking birds' eggs just to put them in a glass case is an awful thing to do. No, I wanted to try to hatch it.'

'He's mad on birds,' put in Jack's father. 'Got a way with them, he has.'

'Just a moment, Mr Daw,' said the Director. 'Let me get this straight,' and to Jack he said, 'You didn't, of course.'

'Didn't what?'

'Didn't succeed in hatching it?'

'Yes,' said Jack, 'I did. Well, one of my geese did.

I call him Oliver. He's a year old now, nearly a year and a quarter.'

'He?' said the Director. 'How d'you know it's a cock bird?'

'Well, I didn't really when he was little,' said Jack. 'I just had a feeling he was. But lately his feathers have darkened a lot. Another few months and I reckon he'll be black-and-white. And he's started to boom. It sounds just like it said in the book.'

'And what was that?'

'Like the distant roar of a lion but without the terminal grunt.'

'Quite the expert, aren't we?' said the Director. A cunning look came into his foxy eyes.

'So you're telling me,' he said, 'that you are the owner of a specimen of the African Somali Ostrich, *Struthio molybdophanes?*'

'No,' said Jack. 'Oliver is a North African Ostrich, *Struthio camelus.*'

' 'Strewth!' said the Director.

Just for a moment he looked more human than vulpine.

'The point is,' said Farmer Daw, 'that Jack is not the owner. He took the egg, and so the bird that hatched from it is not his property but yours. I'll give you my address and then you'd better collect it.'

The Director pulled again at his ginger beard.

'I'll come and have a look at him,' he said.

'When?' said Jack.

'Tomorrow.'

*

'Tomorrow,' said Jack to Oliver in the stable that evening. Lydia and Wilfred had been pestered by the goslings to allow their big brother to sleep in the old shed with them, but Jack had not thought it a good idea: apart from the hazard of his big feet, Oliver had grown another six inches.

'Tomorrow they're going to come and take you away from me.'

Oliver turned his head and gazed into his eyes, puzzled perhaps by his sad tone. Jack scratched the top of the ostrich's head. Probably for the last time, he thought. There was a lump in his throat.

There was a lump in Oliver's throat too – his supper.

Jack watched as the bolus, the size of a cricket ball, slipped slowly down the long neck, and his spirits fell with it.

When he woke next day, he wished, for the first time in his life, that he was going to school that Monday morning. It was cowardly, he knew, but that way he would miss all of it – the last goodbyes, the sight of Oliver being caught by the rangers that the Director would bring with him, with a net that probably would frighten him, and then being bundled into a van or a lorry, very likely with his legs tied together so that he could not kick, and being driven away. If he was at school, he wouldn't have to see any of that or hear Oliver's loud '*Hrup!*'s of anger and distress.

But it was half-term.

He dressed and went to let out his birds.

Obedient as always, Oliver followed him from the stable into the orchard, and waited expectantly as Jack opened the door of the old shed under the apple tree.

'Ollie! Ollie! Ollie!' shouted the goslings excitedly, and Lydia said, 'Good morning, Oliver darling. Would you like to take the children for a walk?'

'Yes please, Mama,' said Oliver eagerly.

'Watch out for foxes, lad!' shouted Wilfred. 'They'll get a kick out of meeting you!' and he waddled off, cackling loudly at his own wit.

What a happy family they are now, thought Jack. I'm not the only one who's going to miss Oliver dreadfully.

At breakfast the Daw family was not a happy one.

Jack was silent and played with his food, and the others, including Margery, were miserable on his behalf.

'He's taking it hard,' said Mrs Daw afterwards, when Jack had gone out to the orchard again.

'My fault really,' said Farmer Daw. 'I should have made him return Oliver when he was still a chick.'

'We could take Jack to visit him, at the Wildlife Park, couldn't we?' asked Margery, but before they could answer, they heard a car drive into the yard outside.

Jack heard it too, but when he ran to the orchard gate and saw that it was not a lorry or a van but a red sports car, he heaved a sigh of relief and went back to Oliver. By now the eight goslings, their walk finished, were swimming on the pond with their parents, and Jack and Oliver stood alone together, the boy's arm round the bird's neck.

Then Farmer Daw came into the orchard, with a small thin ginger-bearded figure at his side.

'Oh Oliver,' whispered Jack.

He walked forward, the ostrich following, and stopped in front of the Director.

'Hello,' he said in a flat voice. 'This is Oliver.'

'*Boo!*' said Oliver politely. He stretched out his neck and thrust forward his head in a way that to some people might have appeared menacing, but the Director merely reached into his pocket, took something out, and offered it to the bird on the flat of his hand.

Oliver took it, delicately, and swallowed it.

'*Twoo!*' he said.

Jack watched the shape going down Oliver's throat. It looked square.

'What was that?' he said.

'Dog biscuit,' said the Director. 'They like them.

What have you been feeding him on?'

'I started him on chick crumbs,' said Jack, 'but he usually shares the wet mash I make up for the geese and ducks. Barley meal and sharps and flaked maize mostly – I reckon he gets lots of animal protein when he's foraging, worms and beetles and stuff.'

'Good for you,' said the Director. 'You wouldn't have known, but if you feed ostrich chicks on a high protein diet their bodies get too heavy and they end up with bow legs. Now this chap's legs are beautifully straight and strong. In fact he looks a picture. How does he get on with the rest of the poultry?'

'Oh fine,' said Jack, and he called 'Lydia! Wilfred!'

The white geese came up out of the pond and hastened towards him, shouting their names in reply, while the goslings ran to their big brother, crying, 'Ollie! Ollie! Ollie!'

And then Jack and his father between them told the story of yesterday's drama, and how Oliver had slain the fox.

The Director looked thoughtful.

'A kick that can kill a fox could do awful damage to a boy, you know, Mr Daw,' he said.

'Oh Oliver would never hurt Jack!' laughed Farmer Daw. 'He's as obedient as a sheepdog and as quiet as a lamb.'

Then a thought struck him. If the Director was going to take the ostrich away, why was he worrying about Jack getting hurt? If the Director was going to take the ostrich away, why hadn't he come with a van or a lorry?

'If you're going to take the ostrich away –' he said, but the Director interrupted him.

'I'm not,' he said.

'You're not!' cried Jack. 'You mean . . .?'

'I mean that, at the moment, I don't want him. We've got a mature male – his father – and several females and a number of youngish chicks at the Park just now, and a young male like this wouldn't fit in. The hens would bully him, and as for the cock bird, he'd give him a really hard time, injure him badly perhaps. At best, he'd be isolated and miserable. Later on, when he's full grown, I may be able to place him at some other safari park, but for the present, there's only one thing that Oliver needs.'

Jack licked his lips.

'What's that?' he said.

The Director looked directly at him, and a small smile appeared on the ginger-bearded face.

'A good home, Jack,' he said. 'And that, it seems to me, is what he's got.'

CHAPTER 12

Speed Trials

That day, Jack and Oliver were exactly the same height.

After the Director had gone, they stood side by side, and Jack's father measured them.

'Dead equal,' he said. 'Four foot nine. But not for long.'

And how right he was.

On Jack's tenth birthday they were measured again, and Jack had grown an inch. Oliver had grown nine.

On the ostrich's second birthday he and Farmer Daw stood side by side, and Jack measured them.

'Dead equal,' he said. 'Six feet. But not for long.'

There was no doubt now that Oliver was a male. Like all his kind, his long neck and his strong legs with their heavily-muscled thighs were bare of feathers, but those on his body were now coal-black, contrasting strikingly with the snowy-white of wing- and tail-plumes.

Somehow, since the Director's visit to the farm, Jack had come to terms with the fact that Oliver was only to be his for a limited time. One day the ostrich would have to go, but in the meantime Jack determined simply to enjoy his company. And though Oliver was his favourite, he did not neglect all his other feathered pets. Jack in fact had become something of a dealer in birds, for such was his success as a breeder, of budgerigars and bantams in particular, that he earned himself a nice bit of pocket money by selling surplus stock.

Lydia and Wilfred's first eight goslings made him a handsome profit when they were old enough to be sold, and by then Lydia had hatched a second brood to run happily about with the giant childminder.

But now Oliver not only minded them, but began occasionally to treat them to the full courting display of the mature male ostrich. After a series of loud 'BOOM!'s he would sink down, flapping his wings wildly, and whipping his head from side to side across the grass on the end of that long neck. Why he did this, Oliver did not know, and nor did the goslings, but they much enjoyed the show and would applaud it with loud cries of, 'Ollie! Ollie! Ollie!'

Jack knew of course – Oliver needed a mate, needed his own flock of hen ostriches; and Jack also knew that, when the chance came for the ostrich to have them, he must, though he should feel sorry for himself, be happy for Oliver. But still he dreaded a summons from the Wildlife Park.

Then one evening the phone rang and Jack answered it.

'Is that Jack Daw?' said a voice.

'Yes.'

'How's Oliver?'

Jack knew straightaway who it was. The voice was not deep enough for the police sergeant, and only one other person knew Oliver's name. He gulped.

'He's OK,' he said. This is it, he thought.

'Good,' said the Director. 'I'm ringing you in case you hadn't noticed that there's a wildlife programme tonight all about ostriches. 8.30. BBC 2.'

'Oh thanks!' said Jack.

'Right,' said the Director. 'Cheerio then, Jack,' and he rang off without another word.

The programme was partly about wild ostriches,

and partly about ostrich farming in South Africa, where the birds were raised in large numbers, to be slaughtered for their feathers, for their meat and for their skins which were made into a kind of leather. Jack didn't like this part of it at all, but what he did like was the closing sequence. This was about ostrich racing.

The runners were cock birds, each guided by his jockey with reins attached to a kind of halter, and away they all went at tremendous speed.

'Look at that!' said Jack.

'Don't you get any ideas,' said his mother.

'You'd fall off anyway,' said his sister.

'Oliver wouldn't let you get on,' said his father.

But Oliver did.

The very next day, without telling the others, Jack went out to the orchard, where Oliver was grazing at the far end. At Jack's call, he came cruising up and stood looking down at the boy, fluttering his eyelashes. Lately, Jack had not been able to give the ostrich his favourite head-scratching because Oliver was now so tall, and the bird, sensing this, would bend his neck for it. This he now did, but Jack did not comply. Instead he folded his legs beneath him and sat down on the grass. At the same time he patted the ground and said, 'Sit!'

Oliver remained standing.

Jack had expected this, and now took from his pocket one of the large square dog-biscuits which, ever since the Director's visit, he had been buying as special treats.

'Sit!' he said again, but although Oliver nuzzled hopefully at the hand that held the biscuit, Jack would not release it.

At last, perhaps by chance, perhaps out of companionship, perhaps because he was tired of standing up, Oliver sat down, and was given his reward. Jack made no further move that morning. Like all good animal trainers, he knew that patience was a must, and not until a week later, when he was confident that Oliver would sit on command, did he get to his feet beside the sitting bird, and slowly, casually, head-scratching all the time, put one leg across Oliver's back, just for a moment, and then take it away again.

Each day he straddled the sitting ostrich a little longer, and then began to put a little weight on his back, gradually, until at last the moment came when he was resting his whole weight on Oliver.

Jack waited, not knowing what to expect.

Would Oliver '*Hrup!*' at him in displeasure?

Would he jump up and chuck him off?

Or would he just go on sitting there, as he had been told to do?

Oliver did none of these things.

To Jack's delight he rose easily to his feet and began to walk down the orchard like any trained riding-ostrich.

From then on it was easy. To ride Oliver was, for Jack, the greatest fun, and he very soon realized that, for Oliver, it was a pleasant task to carry him.

Within a week they had progressed from a walk to a gentle trot. Oliver held his head high, his neck curved back like a swan's, and Jack sat easily on his back, gripping the bird's body with his knees and balancing himself by holding lightly with his hands on either side of the thick throat. A tap with the heels increased Oliver's speed, and a hand signal – one or other arm held out sideways – turned him to left or to right.

There was only one thing wrong, to Jack's mind. They couldn't go fast enough. Oliver was so conditioned to watching where he put his big feet, for fear of stepping on goslings, that he could not be persuaded to run at speed, which Jack was longing for him to do.

Lydia and Wilfred watched these antics from different points of view. Lydia was no longer astonished at anything that Oliver did. Raising two broods of goslings had convinced her that, whatever he was, he was not of the same species. He was a changeling.

Wilfred however clung stubbornly to his belief that his son, despite everything, was a gander.

He watched rider and steed with pride.

'Remarkable fellow, that lad of ours,' he said to Lydia. 'Carrying the boy on his back! You wouldn't believe any goose could do such a thing, would you?'

'No,' said Lydia.

That evening, when the family was swimming on the duckpond, Oliver came up for a drink.

'Come on in, Ollie!' shouted the new goslings. 'The water's lovely!'

For the first time for ages Oliver remembered Lydia's words of long ago. 'You mustn't go into that pond again until you're much bigger,' she had said.

Oliver looked down at his feet. I *am* much bigger, he thought, and he walked gingerly, one slow stride at a time, into the pond. The day had been a hot one, and Oliver waded deeper, enjoying the pleasant sensation of the cool water on his legs, legs now so long that even in the deepest part his body was still above the surface.

He moved around the middle of the pond, and Wilfred cried loudly, 'Well done, lad, you're swimming at last! You wouldn't believe it, Lydia, would you?'

'No,' said Lydia.

Next day Jack got up very early. The time had come, he reckoned, for speed trials, and he did not want anyone to see them.

As the police sergeant had said, the Daws' farm was pretty isolated, and even the nearest country lane was some way away. From it a tarmac farm road led to the house and buildings, and it was along this farm road that Jack planned to give Oliver his head. Sensibly though, he made the first trial on grass.

'That road is hard, you see,' he said to Oliver, as he walked him out of the stable, 'and I might fall off when you get into top gear.'

But in fact he found that the faster Oliver went, the easier it was to ride him, so smooth was that huge flowing stride. The ostrich seemed to know what was expected of him, and they raced across the biggest of the pastures at a fine rate.

'Now,' said Jack, 'get your breath, Oliver, because this is the real trial. The farm road is exactly half a mile long – I made a note of it on the trip in Dad's car the other day – so I can work out your top speed.'

Neither '*Boo!*' '*Twoo!*' or '*Hrup!*' really served as an answer when Oliver, as now, did not understand what

Jack was on about, but he was fired up by the thrill of a good gallop and he sensed that something challenging was about to happen, so he gave a loud 'BOOM!'

Jack rode to the junction of the farm road with the lane, looked cautiously to make sure there was no one about, and then turned the ostrich's head towards the stable. He waited until the second hand on his watch reached 12, and then, with a dig of his heels, he cried, 'Go, Oliver! Go!'

And how Oliver went!

His giant strides ate up the ground, and the cows in the neighbouring field stampeded and buck-jumped wildly as Jack flashed by on his great black-and-white charger.

Somehow he managed to keep his eye on the face of the watch as they sailed through the farm gate, the finishing line, and he saw that the second hand pointed to 9. They had covered the half-mile in exactly 45 seconds.

Ten minutes later, after much chewing on a stub of pencil, and many crossed-out sums on the back of an old envelope, he came up with the answer: 40 m.p.h.!

He had to tell the family, of course, he couldn't possibly keep it to himself any longer, and that afternoon, after school, he repeated the run, while they all stood at the gate and goggled in amazement.

His mother spoke for all of them when she said, 'I simply don't believe my eyes!'

'I'll do it again,' said Jack, and he walked Oliver back to the start.

But on this next run Oliver had just reached full speed when Jack suddenly heard, behind him on the farm road, the sound of a car and, glancing back, saw it following him.

A red sports car it was, and at the wheel was a small thin figure, with a narrow face and a ginger beard.

CHAPTER 13

Time Flies

'I simply don't believe my eyes!' said the Director to the Daws.

He got out of the red car and walked to meet rider and steed as they came trotting back.

'Hullo, Jack,' he said.

'Hullo,' said Jack, nervously.

'And hullo, Oliver.'

'*Boo-hoo-hoo-hoo*,' said Oliver, breathlessly.

'D'you know how fast you were going?' said the Director.

'About forty, I expect.'

'You expect right. How long have you been riding him?'

'About a week. But I haven't let him go full out before. Today's the first time.'

'And the last, I'm afraid,' said the Director.

He turned to Farmer Daw.

'No point in mincing words, Mr Daw,' he said. 'I came to tell you that I need this ostrich. Our cock bird – his father – is getting on a bit now and so are his hens. I'm sending them all to a safari park that's just starting up, at the other end of the country.

We're going to begin again with fresh blood, some new young hens that I've imported. And a new young male.'

'Oliver,' said Jack.

' 'Fraid so,' said the Director. 'Quite apart from the fact that I need him, he needs to be with his own kind, you know. Ostriches are flock birds, and it's not natural for him to be on his own.'

'I know,' said Jack. 'He's been displaying a lot lately, and booming much more too. Anyway, he isn't really mine. The egg belonged to you.'

He scratched the top of the ostrich's head.

'In some ways Oliver will always be yours,' said the Director. 'I've thought a lot about this, and though I don't see that we need to pay you money for him – strictly speaking he belongs to the Wildlife Park – we certainly need to compensate you. You've done a tremendous job, Jack, to hatch and rear such a magnificent specimen. The least I can do is to give you a Life Membership card. That means that you can visit the Park, free of charge, whenever you want to.'

'You'll still be able to see Oliver as often as you like,' said Jack's mother.

'Thank you very much,' said Jack.

I just wish I'd had longer to ride him, he thought.

'I expect you wish you'd had longer to ride him,' said the Director.

'Yes.'

The Director smiled.

'We might be able to arrange that,' he said. 'Perhaps every now and then your dad could bring you over early, before we open to the public?'

Farmer Daw smiled.

'We might be able to arrange that,' he said.

The actual parting wasn't as dreadful as Jack had feared. They sent a cattle lorry, so that there would be enough headroom for Oliver to stand comfortably, and Jack persuaded him up the ramp, and was waiting at the Wildlife Park to off-load him.

Oliver walked sedately down, and looked around, and saw, out in the ostrich paddock, a number of strange birds. His great eyes widened, as he stared at them in amazement.

Those birds are not like Mama and Papa, he thought.

But I am not like Mama and Papa, he thought.

Those birds, he thought, are like me!

With the loudest 'BOOM!' he had ever boomed, he ran to meet them.

The Director and Farmer Daw and Jack stood watching as Oliver reached his hens. He sank down before them, flapping his wings wildly, and whipping his head from side to side across the grass on the end of that long neck, while each hen ostrich pretended to take no notice but slyly watched the handsome stranger out of the corner of her eye.

'He's happy,' said Jack quietly. 'Let's go home.'

'You'll be able to see him again soon,' said his father.

'Time flies,' said the Director. 'You'd be surprised.'

Time flew, and Jack was indeed surprised one day when, looking through the diary in which he recorded all the hatchings of all his many different birds, he realized that Lydia and Wilfred's present brood of goslings was their seventh! Five years had flashed by since Oliver had left the farm, five years during which Jack had visited him, and his wives, and his many children, as often as possible, sometimes early, for a ride.

Absence makes the heart grow fonder, they say, and the bond between boy and bird was even stronger.

One day he arrived to be told that he was wanted in the Director's office.

When he went in, there was a smile on the foxy face.

'You're taller every time I see you,' said the Director. 'How much d'you reckon you've grown since first we met?'

'About a foot, I should think,' said Jack.

'Oliver must have grown three feet in that same time,' said the Director. 'Thanks to him – and thanks to you in the first place, of course – we've got a splendid flock of ostriches here now. It's really getting a bit too much for the ranger who looks after them on top of his other work. He needs someone to help him, someone who could eventually take over the ostriches.'

Jack said nothing. His heart was going like a trip-hammer.

The Director put up a paw and pulled at that ginger beard, flecked now with grey.

'You'll be leaving school soon?' he said.

'Yes.'

'Want a job?'

CHAPTER 14

And How!

Beside the ostrich paddock at the Wildlife Park a party of schoolchildren was standing, ceaselessly nagging their teacher to allow them to open their packed lunches. ('I'm starving, Miss, it's more than two hours since I had my breakfast.')

It was the middle of the morning, and fixed to the wire fence beside the information notice was another, that said

---
DEMONSTRATION OF OSTRICH RIDING
10.30 a.m.

A lot of people now began to collect, and then, sharp at half past ten, they were joined by one of the Park rangers. Quite a young chap he seemed, not much more than a boy really, but he called out confidently 'Ladies and Gentlemen!' and when he had the crowd's attention, he said 'Good morning, everyone. My name is Jack Daw, and in a moment I'm going to ride our big male ostrich. But before I do, I must warn you all, the younger ones especially, that this is not something that anyone can do. A kick from an ostrich can kill a man. The only reason that I'm able to ride our cock bird is that I brought him up. I put an ostrich egg under a goose – just as a cuckoo lays her egg in the nest of a hedge sparrow or a wagtail – and that goose hatched out this cuckoo child. And I reared him till he was two years old. Now he's eight, and he weighs 345 pounds, and he stands exactly nine feet tall.'

Then the young ranger unlocked a wire gate in the fencing, and went in, closing it behind him, and cupped his hands to his mouth and called, 'Ol–i–ver!'

In reply there came a noise like the roar of a distant lion, and the people saw a great black-and-white bird half as tall again as a man leave his smaller greyish wives, and come striding across the grass, and stop and stand beside the ranger, staring down at him out of huge brown eyes.

'*Boo!*' said the giant bird softly.

Then it bent its neck for the ranger to scratch the top of its head.

'*Twoo!*' said Oliver. '*Twoo! Twoo!*' and he fluttered his eyelashes.

'Sit!' said Jack, and Oliver sat, and waited till the jockey was mounted.

Then he rose to his full height and began to walk away with long slow deliberate strides to the far side of the paddock.

Here, bird and rider stopped and turned, and stood for a long moment as still as stone, silhouetted against the summer sky.

Then, just as the crowd was beginning to think

nothing more would happen, they heard the ranger cry, 'Go, Oliver! Go!'

And then how they clapped and cheered!

And how the mighty ostrich ran!

And how still and proud upon his great back sat Jack Daw, who had a way with birds!

And how!

WITHDRAWN
FROM THE COLLECTION OF
WINDSOR PUBLIC LIBRARY